PALETERO MAN

by Latin Grammy winner
LUCKY DIAZ

illustrated by
MICAH PLAYER

HARPER
An Imprint of HarperCollinsPublishers

Paletero Man • Text copyright © 2021 by Lucky Diaz • Illustrations copyright © 2021 by Micah Player • All rights reserved. Printed in the United States of America. • No part of this book may be used or reproduced in any manner whatsoever without written permission except in the case of brief quotations embodied in critical articles and reviews. For information address HarperCollins Children's Books, a division of HarperCollins Publishers, 195 Broadway, New York, NY 10007. • www.harpercollinschildrens.com • ISBN 978-0-06-301444-2 • The artist used Adobe Photoshop to create the digital illustrations for this book. • Typography by Chelsea C. Donaldson • 21 22 23 24 25 PC 10 9 8 7 6 5 4 3 2 ❖ First Edition

To Alisha. The dreamiest of dreamers.—L.D.

For my mom, lover of words and hider of the good ice cream.

Sorry for all the times I found it.—M.P.

In the hottest month,
on the hottest day,
in the city of Dreamers,
California—LA,

I grab my dinero
and make my way
to find my friend
Paletero José!

Pushing his cart
full of cool treats,
bailando, he dances
to mariachi beats.

He has dozens of flavors.
Mmm—I can already taste.

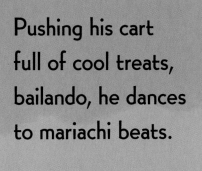

Will he have my favorite?
There's not a second to waste!

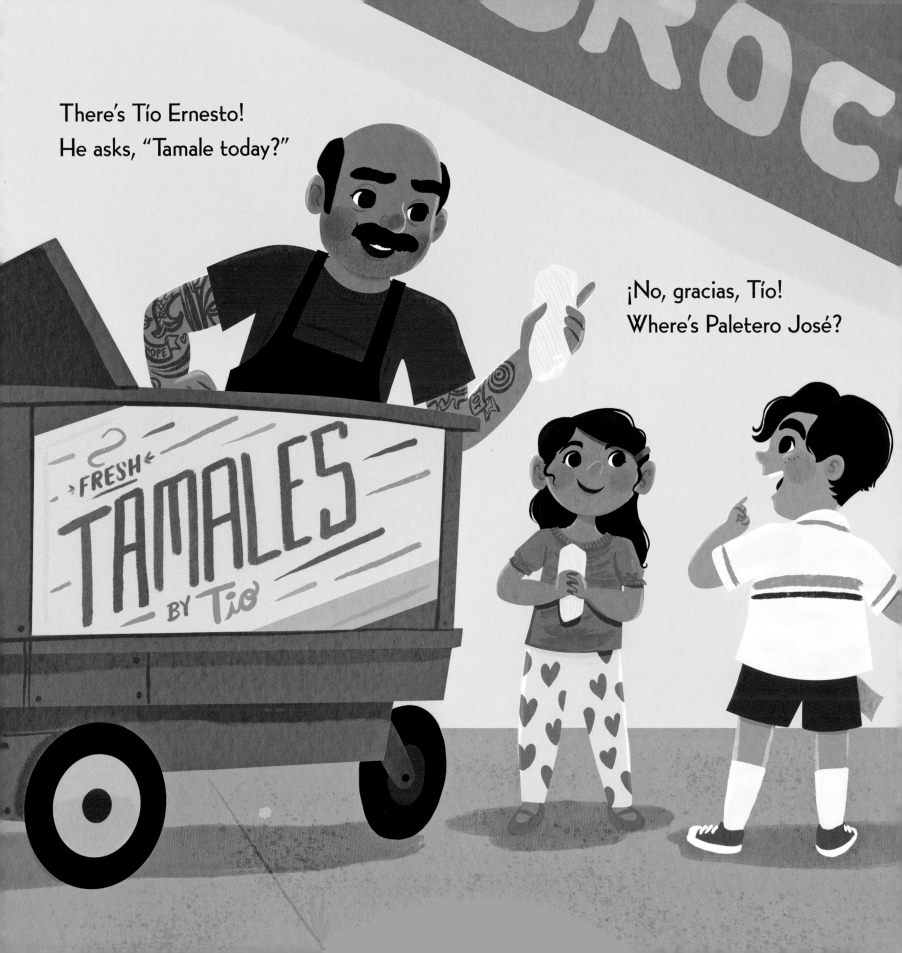

There's Tío Ernesto!
He asks, "Tamale today?"

¡No, gracias, Tío!
Where's Paletero José?

"RING! RING! RING!"

Can you hear his call?

Paletas for one!
Paletas for all!

Un aroma is calling,
caught in the breeze.
It's a BBQ smell
coming from Ms. Lee's!

RING! RING! RING!

Can you hear his call?
Paletas for one!
Paletas for all!

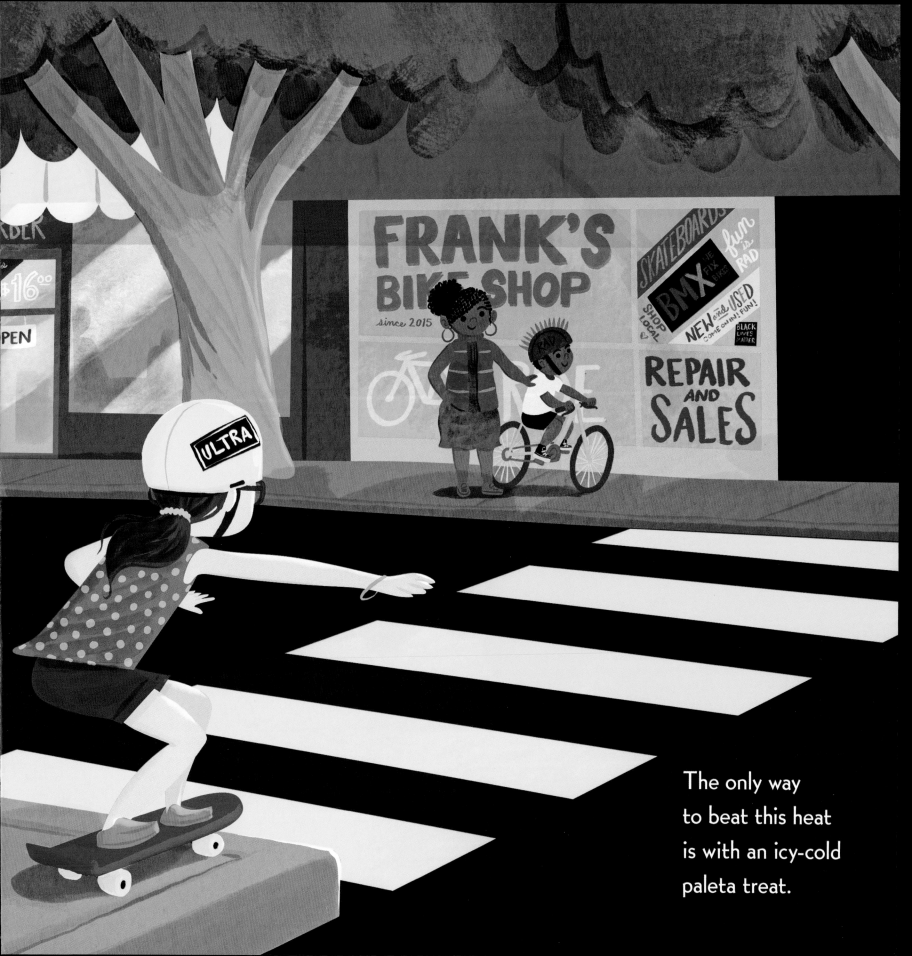

The only way
to beat this heat
is with an icy-cold
paleta treat.

There's my friend
from the bike shop.

Lo siento, Frank.
There's no time to stop!

"RING!
RING!
RING!"

Can you hear his call?
Paletas for one!
Paletas for all!

Will he have all the flavors,
the colors I love?
Horchata, canela,
the kind I dream of.

¿Chocolate, elote,
sandía, o fresa,
arroz con leche,
miel, o cereza?

"RING!"

RING!

RING!

Can you hear his call?
Paletas for one!
Paletas for all!

Here he is!
Paletero José!
Finally, I'll get cool
on this very hot day!

¡Oye, niños!
What will it be?

He has all my favorites!
Can it be true?
¡Chocolate, vainilla,
y melón, too!

But today I'd like piña.
Do you have that sabor?
He smiles a big smile—
"¡Claro! Para ti, ¡el mejor!"

I reach into my pocket
to pay for my paleta . . .

¡Mi dinero! My money!
¡Está perdido!
It's missing. It's lost!
¿A dónde se ha ido?

What will I do?
What can I say?
How can I buy
my paleta today?

And just at that moment,
who do I see?
My neighborhood friends,
Tío, Frank, and Ms. Lee.

"We called out your name
when we saw your coins drop,
but you must have not heard us,
because you didn't stop."

Muchas gracias, amigos.
What would I have done?
I guess I dropped my money
when I was on the run.

"Kindness for all!"
shouts Paletero José.
"I have a surprise
that will brighten your day.

"Oye, amigos—
paletas on me.
Because of your kindness
the paletas are free!

"Whether it's stormy
or whether it's sunny,
whether or not
you have any money,

"I'll always help out an amigo in need.

Yo te prometo—

an amigo indeed!"

In the hottest month,
on the hottest day,
we have fun in the sun
with Paletero José.

"RING! RING! RING!"

We can hear his call!
Paletas for one!
Paletas for all!

Author's Note

The smell of street tacos, the vivid rainbow colors of vendor umbrellas, and the sounds of children choosing their favorite flavor from the paletero cart on a Saturday afternoon. These are some of the sights and sounds of Eighth Street in Los Angeles. My neighborhood, my home, and my inspiration for *Paletero Man*—the book and song.

Spanning the neighborhoods from Koreatown to Boyle Heights, Eighth Street has endless numbers of taquerias, K-town BBQs, colorful murals, and vendor-lined streets. This historic stretch is also the birthplace of the immigrant street food vending culture in Los Angeles. Snack trips to the elotero cart (Mexican street corn), visits to our friend selling tamales out of her cooler on the corner, and, of course, weekend paletas in the park really shape our lives and fill our stomachs.

As a Mexican American and an Angeleno, I've taken great pride and joy in writing and sharing this picture book with you. And as a Chicanx parent, being able to celebrate our vibrant culture and read this book with my daughter is really the most special experience of all.

I hope you taste and imagine the fun of choosing your own refreshing paleta when reading *Paletero Man*.

Buen provecho,

Lucky Diaz